Nut,
Sky goddess

Shu, Air god

Anubis,
god
of the
Under-
world

Thoth,
god of
Scribes

Geb, Earth god

Ammit,
the Great
Devourer

Osiris,
god
of the
Dead

Hathor,
goddess
of Love

Nepthys,
sister of Isis

Apshai
insect

Horus,
Sun god

Crocodile

Isis, wife of Osiris

Underworld

THE WINGED CAT

THE WINGED CAT

A Tale of Ancient Egypt

DEBORAH NOURSE LATTIMORE

HarperCollins*Publishers*

To Erica Denise Silverman, friend and writer

The Winged Cat: A Tale of Ancient Egypt
Copyright © 1992 by Deborah Nourse Lattimore
Printed in the U.S.A.
Typography by Al Cetta
1 2 3 4 5 6 7 8 9 10
First Edition

Library of Congress Cataloging-in-Publication Data
Lattimore, Deborah Nourse.
   The winged cat : a tale of ancient Egypt / Deborah Nourse
Lattimore.
      p.   cm.
   Summary: In ancient Egypt, a young servant girl and a High Priest
must each find the correct magic spells from the Book of the Dead
that open the twelve gates of the Netherworld to determine who is
telling the truth about the death of the girl's sacred cat.
   ISBN 0-06-023635-3. — ISBN 0-06-023636-1 (lib. bdg.)
   [1. Egypt—Fiction.   2. Cats—Fiction.   3. Magic—Fiction.]
I. Title.
PZ7.L36998Wi   1992   90-38441
[Fic]—dc20   CIP
                                                             AC

In Egypt most ancient there lived a serving girl named Merit who worked in the temple of the cat goddess Bastet. When she swept the halls in the heat of day, her friend Bast, a small cat, kept her company. At night, when Merit's work was done, they strolled out to sleep in cool comfort on the sandy banks of the Nile.

On just such a night, across the moonlit sky, the god Thoth sailed to the Netherworld, his home. Silently, as he traveled the starry stream, something fell from his neck down, far down, and landed between the sleeping girl and the cat.

The next morning Waha, Pharaoh's High Priest, spotted it. It was a gold amulet shaped like a heart, and there was nothing Waha loved more than gold. He carefully stepped over the sleeping girl and picked it up. Merit awoke but kept her eyes shut, because she recognized the voice of the powerful High Priest. His bad temper was well known.

"This is very royal indeed," Merit heard him say. "Should I take it to Pharaoh, or should I keep it?" As he turned to go, Waha tripped over Bast the cat, and the golden heart flew into the river.

"You! You rat-chasing lump of fur!" shouted Waha angrily. He seized Bast and flung her downstream.

Merit jumped up and rushed into the current to save Bast. But it was too late. The cat was lifeless in her arms.

"Pharaoh will judge you harshly for this!" cried Merit. "This poor cat belonged to the temple of the goddess Bastet."

"Go to Pharaoh, worm of a girl," retorted Waha. "See for yourself if a stupid cat matters at all."

Merit told Pharaoh what had happened, and the High Priest soon found himself called to the foot of the throne.

"A sacred cat was drowned," said Pharaoh. "Merit says you did it. You swear you did not. I cannot decide who is telling the truth."

"You have only to look into my heart to see that I am telling the truth," Waha said.

"Your words inspire my command," said Pharaoh. "Hear me! You must each take the magic spells from the Book of the Dead and travel to the Netherworld. When you arrive in the Hall of Judgment, the gods will decide who is telling the truth. If your heart weighs the same as Ma'at, the feather of Truth, you will have nothing to fear. But if your heart weighs more, it will be proof that you are lying, and the monster Ammit will devour you. Go and prepare!"

Now even though Waha was the High Priest, he did not own the necessary spells because he had sold them for gold. So he scribbled the few spells he remembered onto small wooden figures called *ushabtis*. If the spells were the right ones, he could use them to open the twelve gates of the Netherworld. If the spells were wrong, he could always throw an *ushabti* to a hungry demon and still be safe.

Merit returned to the temple of Bastet. She took the limp body of Bast, wrapped it in fine linen, and laid food and drink before it.

"Farewell, dear Bast," Merit said sadly. "Waha will find his way, and I, without any spells, will be lost and monsters will eat me."

"*I* will not say farewell," said Bast.

"What!" exclaimed Merit. "You can speak?"

"My *ba*-soul speaks," answered Bast. "I was living my fourth life when that fool of a High Priest tripped over me and tossed me into the river. Now I must travel to the Netherworld to get my next life. Since you were kind enough to give me such a fine funeral, I will go with you."

"But I am too poor to buy spells from the Book of the Dead," said Merit. "How will we find the way?"

"The Book of the Dead is much more than just a handful of spells," purred Bast. "Spells are words. If you can read, we will find our way. Remember. Unless you keep your eyes ahead of you and read, all will be lost."

That evening as the sun blazed its path beyond the Western Horizon, Waha stood on the shore. Merit, with the invisible soul of Bast the cat on her shoulder, stood beside him. A gleaming boat appeared. On its deck stood the sun god, Horus, surrounded by the rays of the setting sun.

"Look carefully!" whispered Bast. "See the words? Read them and the boat will take us to the twelve gates of the Netherworld."

Merit saw hidden words appear, and she read them aloud.

"The mooring pin is like two ladies. They are Upper and Lower Egypt," she began. "The sails are bigger than Heaven. That is the goddess Nut. The oars are a hawk's fingers, and that is Horus. The breeze that holds up the sky is Shu. The ground is Geb, and the river is H'apy, the Nile."

"Come ride on my boat," said Horus, beckoning to Merit. "Now it is the Priest's turn."

Waha searched frantically in his sack. He finally brought out one *ushabti* and squinted at it.

"I have forgotten what this says," he muttered.

"Then feed the demon or be devoured," said Horus.

Waha threw a *ushabti* behind the boat to a demon, who gobbled it up with terrible gnashing teeth. Bast spread her wings around Merit's head so she would not look. Waha looked, and suddenly he remembered the heart amulet that had started the whole dispute. He stared into the water hoping to find it.

The boat stopped at the first of the twelve gates. Waha fished with his fingers behind the stern. Merit looked up. The great gate was staring at her.

"Name my parts and you may pass," it said.

Merit shook, hand to arm, knee to leg, as hungry monsters crowded around the boat, hoping she would make a mistake. She eyed the door carefully, and pictures appeared. Merit spoke:

"On the lintel is the great vulture who protects all Egypt. The side posts are legs and a cup, and on the door is a hand."

The door opened a crack, and then it stopped and looked at Waha. The High Priest dug around in his sack but could not find what he needed. Quickly he tossed another *ushabti* behind the boat, and Merit heard the crunching of giant teeth. Waha leaned back and ran his fingers through the water in search of the amulet.

One by one Merit called out the names of the great doors, and one by one they opened. Waha made more and more mistakes and threw more and more of his *ushabtis* to the demons.

Finally, Waha became impatient. "Why must I make this dangerous journey just to rid myself of a stupid worm of a girl?" he thought. He leaned over in time to see the golden heart floating beside the boat. Quickly he plucked it from the water and thrust it into his sack. Now he had what he wanted. All he had to do was rid himself of Merit and go home.

The sun boat stopped at the entrance to the Hall of Judgment. On either side were swirling pits of fire. Just as Merit stepped out of the boat, Waha shoved her into the flames.

"Oh, no! Bast! Help me!" Merit cried.

"Stop! Think!" said Bast, spreading her wings around Merit's head. *"Read!"*

Through the flames, Merit could see on the doorway above her the words of the last spell:

"May this magic fire burn me if I am not good in my heart!"

As she spoke the words, the fires parted. Merit was saved.

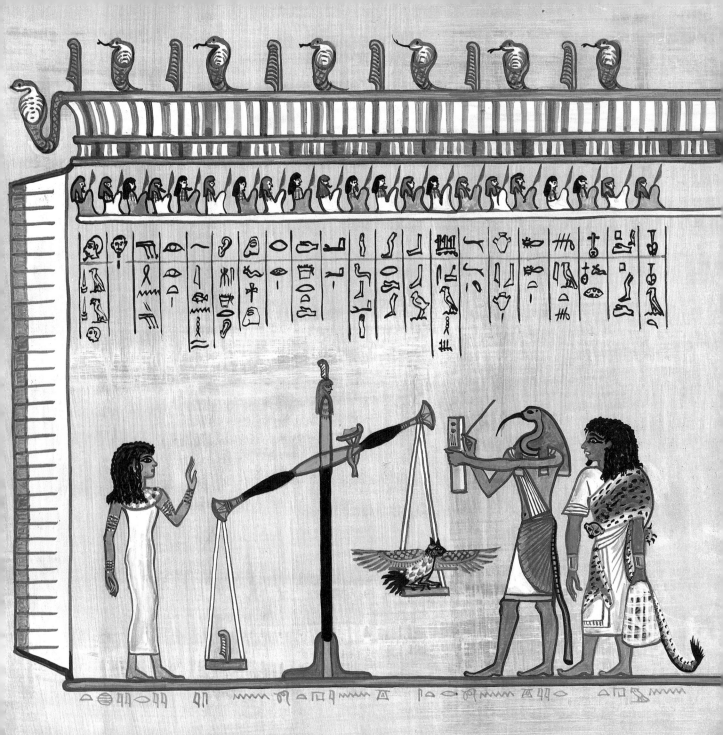

"Approach!" called a voice from the end of the Hall.

It was Anubis, the jackal-headed god of the dead. He stood beside the giant scales of Truth. Thoth stood on the other side, ready to record the results with ink reed and papyrus. Ammit crouched at the base of the scales grinding his teeth. Behind them all, staring in disbelief, was Waha.

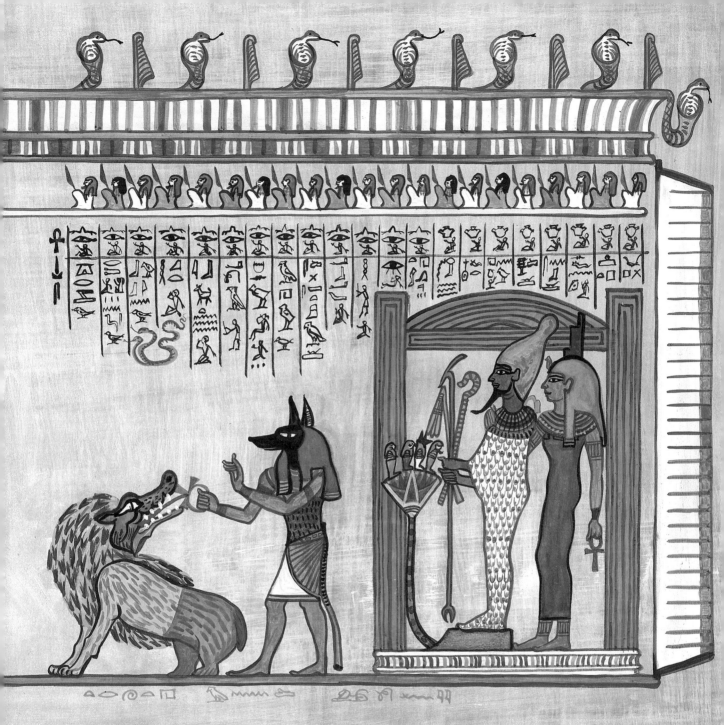

"We know why you have come," said Anubis. "Since Merit passed the test of fire, she is now free. And Bast—let your *ba*-soul and heart be weighed against the feather of Truth and you may gain another life."

Bast flew to the scales. Since it was a soul and heart with cat wings, it was lighter than the feather. The scale tipped up.

"By Bes!" laughed Waha. "That's nothing! Why, I have something here much better than that!"

Waha produced the golden heart amulet and gave it to Anubis to put on the scales. The heart, in its shining beauty, sank to the ground like the metal that it was.

"Guilty!" said Thoth. "Furthermore, I've been looking for this!"

Thoth picked up the heart and returned it to his neck. And before anyone could say "By Bes!" twice, Ammit had chewed and swallowed all of Waha, right down to his last *ushabti*.

As for Bast and Merit, they were taken on Horus's golden boat back to the riverbanks of the Nile. When Pharaoh saw them, he knew at once whose hearts

were as good as gold. He rewarded Merit with a life of ease and plenty.

Bast even lived four more.

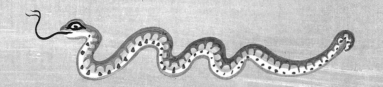

AFTERWORD

The ancient Egyptians loved life and believed that after people died, they lived again in a beautiful garden called The Field of Rushes. It had a river and marshes, fields, and fish and fowl. In fact, it looked just like Egypt itself. So eager were the ancient Egyptians to be sure that life after death was just like life itself, they had all their favorite things buried with them: clothes, food, perfumes, makeup, beds, chests of linens and jewels, and magic amulets to protect them from snakes and bugs. To do all the farming, cooking, and cleaning they included little wooden figures called *ushabtis* which often looked just like the dead person and did all the work so that he or she wouldn't have to. Even the dead person's body was supposed to stay as close as possible to its appearance in life. After death, the internal organs were removed and placed in special containers called canopic jars. The body was piled high with natron crystals, a kind of salt, and dried out until it looked a lot like leather. Then it was wrapped in fine linen, given a funeral complete with mourners, dancers and priests, and offerings of bread, beer and meat and fowl. (Since the new mummy couldn't really eat, the mourners did.) Then, with all of his or her possessions placed around the coffin, the deceased was sealed up in a tomb for eternity, life everlasting.

There was just one catch. The dead person had to go to the Netherworld, home of the gods and goddesses, to be judged worthy of a new life. A dead person's *ba*, or winged soul, went before forty-two Judges and was asked questions such as, "Did you do any good deeds while you were alive? What were they?" If the soul

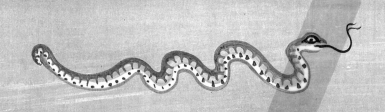

answered correctly, then its heart was weighed on a scale against the feather *Ma'at* (Truth), and if the heart weighed less, the *ba* was free to go. But if the heart weighed more, a terrible demon called Ammit, part crocodile, lion, and hippopotamus, gobbled up the soul and the heart, and the person was gone forever.

Answers, spells, and confessions of good-deed-doing or confessions of wrong-doing were put together on papyrus rolls and buried with the deceased to help him on his way through the Netherworld and its dangers. Spells from different dynasties were collected by Pharaohs; later by nobles and then commoners and were called The Books of the Dead. Egyptologists—scholars who study ancient Egypt—know them as the Amduat, The Coming Out by Day, The Book of Caverns, The Book of Breathings, The Book of the Two Ways, and others. Poor people were buried with a very few spells; the richer you were the more spells you could afford. But whether you were poor or rich, it was your heart that mattered, and the Judges of the Dead could see right through it to the truth.

In THE WINGED CAT such ceremonies as The Opening of the Mouth, the Weighing of the Heart, and the Twelve Portals of the Night (for the twelve hours of the night) are seen on various pages. It would be impossible to include all the adventures a *ba* would encounter in the Netherworld in a single picture book, but anyone wishing to read further should run to the nearest library and look up the Egyptian Books of the Dead. I read many, many sources in English, German,

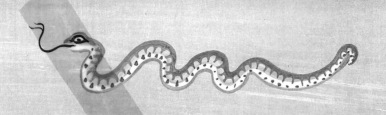

French, and hieroglyphic before I wrote this story. My favorite papyri, primarily from the British Museum, are: BM10470 (the Overseer of the Granaries, Ani); BM10477 (Steward of the Chief Treasurer, Nu); and many others, all of which can be found in R.O. Faulkner's THE ANCIENT EGYPTIAN BOOK OF THE DEAD, revised edition, 1985. For translations I used both Sir Alan Gardiner's EGYPTIAN GRAMMAR and R.O. Faulkner's dictionary.

No curse will befall you for reading this book; rather, as any ancient Egyptian would say, *An'k, wedj', senab'* (Life! Prosperity! Health!) for all time!

—Deborah Nourse Lattimore